DIVERSITY IN ACTION

Diversity in Business

CATHLEEN SMALL

New York

Published in 2019 by The Rosen Publishing Group, Inc.
29 East 21st Street
New York, NY 10010

Copyright © 2019 by The Rosen Publishing Group, Inc.

First Edition

All rights reserved. No part of this book may be reproduced in any form without permission in writing from the publisher, except by a reviewer.

Produced for Rosen by Calcium
Editors for Calcium: Sarah Eason and Jennifer Sanderson
Designer: Simon Borrough
Picture researcher: Rachel Blount

Photo credits: Cover photo of Oprah Winfrey: Shutterstock/J Stone; Inside: Shutterstock: 13_Phunkod: p. 32; Achinthamb: p. 6; Africa Studio: p. 22; ALPA PROD: p. 34; Ryan Rodrick Beiler: pp. 42-43; Olesia Bilkei: p. 35; Paolo Bona: p. 38; Dfree: p. 8; Dragon Images: pp. 3, 11, 17; Karelnoppe: p. 37; Krista Kennell: pp. 14, 20; Vasin Lee: p. 25; Anthony Leousis: p. 28; Ahmet Misirligul: p. 19; Monkey Business Images: pp. 1, 5, 16, 18; Susan Montgomery: p. 9; Monticello: p. 27; Odua Images: p. 7; Rasstock: p. 12; Rawpixel.com: pp. 13, 29, 30, 31; Rvlsoft: p. 21; RyFlip: p. 24; Phil Stafford: p. 40; Superjoseph: p. 41; Sylv1rob1: p. 39; Thanatos Media: p. 36; UfaBizPhoto: p. 10; Ken Wolter: p. 15; Wikimedia Commons: Cpl. Ashton Buckingham: p. 26; Steve Jurvetson: p. 33; J. Howard Miller: p. 4.

Cataloging-in-Publication Data

Names: Small, Cathleen.
Title: Diversity in business / Cathleen Small.
Description: New York : Rosen Central, 2019. | Series: Diversity in action | Includes glossary and index.
Identifiers: ISBN 9781499440850 (pbk.) | ISBN 9781499440867 (library bound)
Subjects: LCSH: Entrepreneurship—Juvenile literature. | New business enterprises—Juvenile literature. | Cultural pluralism—Juvenile literature. | Diversity in the workplace.
Classification: LCC HB615.S63 2019 | DDC 658.1'1—dc23

Manufactured in the United States of America

Contents

Chapter 1	Diversity on the Rise	4
Chapter 2	Racial Diversity in Business	10
Chapter 3	Gender Diversity in Business	16
Chapter 4	Economic and Social Diversity in Business	22
Chapter 5	Cultural Diversity in Business	28
Chapter 6	Diverse Abilities in Business	34

Timeline 44

Glossary 46

For Further Reading 47

Index 48

Chapter 1
Diversity on the Rise

When the United States was first formed, it was a nation of immigrants and indigenous peoples. Native Americans had lived in the region for thousands of years, and the colonists who settled in North America were from England and European and Scandinavian countries. Some came north from what is now Mexico and Central and South America, too.

The United States Workforce

While the United States has always been a mix of people and cultures, the workforce has not always reflected this diversity. For a long time, business in the United States was run by white men. There were niche businesses run by others, of course. Women may have run seamstress shops, and black citizens might have managed restaurants or other facilities that catered only to other black people. However, in terms of big business and corporations, they were, for a long time, run by white men.

Over the past century, though, that has changed. The US workforce has become more diverse as a result of a number of changes.

Posters like this one from 1943 have inspired women to take on challenges in the workplace.

CRITICAL THINKING QUESTION:
What other niche businesses can you think of that minorities, women, and economically disadvantaged people worked at in years past?

Women originally entered the workforce as teachers and nurses, and later as manual laborers during World War II. Today, women work in virtually every field.

Steps to Change

In 1948 the armed forces were desegregated when President Truman issued Executive Order 9981. This ruled that discrimination based on religion, race, color, or natural origin was illegal for members of the armed forces. This did not apply specifically to business, but it set a precedent for diversity. The Civil Rights Act of 1964 was a major step forward in diversifying the business workforce. This act made it illegal for businesses to discriminate against people when hiring or firing them. It applied to both public and private businesses.

In 1987, Secretary of Labor William Brock commissioned a study called Workforce 2000. Workforce 2000 examined the fact that the US workforce was aging and that if the United States did not find a way to replace the workers and businesspeople who would soon be retiring or dying, the United States would face a slump. The report suggested that to continue to prosper, the United States would have to diversify its workforce.

In 2008, CNN Money and the San Jose *Mercury News* began to investigate the fifteen largest technology companies in the Silicon Valley. They wanted to know the diversity of these companies' workforces, but they found that only three of the companies would provide employment data.

Diversity in Business

Diversity Reports

In 2014, though, technology giant Google turned the tide by releasing a diversity report on its workforce. Google now releases such a report annually. In 2017, the report showed that 31 percent of Google's employees were female. However, the Google workforce was largely white (56 percent) or Asian (35 percent), with only 9 percent of employees being a race other than white or Asian. As of 2017, Google is one of only sixteen companies on the Fortune 500 list to release a public report on employee diversity. However, the company is leading other companies to diversify their workforce by being open about their own efforts to improve diversity in their employee pool.

The Importance of Diversity in Business

Diversity in business is important for a number of reasons. Employee diversity helps companies better understand their customers. Most businesses serve a wide variety of customers, and if their employees are nearly all the same race, culture, gender, or socioeconomic background, it is likely that they will have similar viewpoints. For example, a company made up of wealthy people is not very likely to understand the needs of their poor or underprivileged consumers.

Although tech giant Google publishes an annual report detailing its workforce diversity, the company still employs a majority of white men.

Diversity on the Rise

Lack of diversity can also bring bias. People with the same backgrounds tend to have the same biases. While most people would like to believe they are not biased, the truth is that all people have biases. For example, men who have typically worked with all men may have a bias that men are better workers than women. When a business's workforce is diverse, the employees all bring different biases that can be discussed and addressed.

This leads to the next benefit of diversity in business: creativity. People from different backgrounds bring different perspectives to the table, and that can spark new ideas. New ideas often mean growth for the business, which benefits everyone. One such contemporary idea was the Pro Hijab that sportswear brand Nike released. Female Muslims who wear traditional dress wear hijabs, but typically these head coverings have not been particularly sports-friendly. Employees at Nike recognized this issue and designed the lightweight, breathable Pro Hijab for female Muslim athletes.

Brainstorming and decision-making are also improved by a diverse workforce. The different perspectives and backgrounds that a diverse group of employees can bring to the table result in better brainstorming sessions. Ultimately, the decisions made are based on feedback from a variety of people, rather than from a small group that all hold similar viewpoints.

Nike recognized a niche market and capitalized on it: sports-friendly hijabs for Muslim women.

CRITICAL THINKING QUESTION:
Can you think of any biases that people might hold in the workplace?

Diversity in Business

Oprah Winfrey:
Media Mogul

At first glance, Oprah Winfrey seems an unlikely person to become a business magnate. She had a challenging childhood and faced poverty and racism. Hers is perhaps one of the greatest rags-to-riches stories ever told.

Winfrey used her talent for public speaking to build a billion-dollar empire and become one of the most respected celebrities in the world.

Winfrey was the first black multibillionaire in the United States and is considered the richest black person in America. In addition to being rich, Winfrey is also highly regarded by millions around the world. In 2013, she received the Presidential Medal of Freedom from Barack Obama, and she has earned honorary doctorate degrees from Duke University and Harvard University.

Rags to Riches

Winfrey was born to a single mother in rural Mississippi. When her mother left to move north, Winfrey stayed in Kosciusko, Mississippi, to live with her grandmother. They were so poor that Winfrey went to school in dresses made from potato sacks. When Winfrey was six years old, she moved north to live with her mother in Milwaukee, Wisconsin. Winfrey's mother was not as strict as her grandmother, but she was also not as supportive. Winfrey bounced back and forth between her mother's home in Milwaukee and her father's home in Nashville throughout elementary school, middle school, and high school. Like her mother, Winfrey became a teenage single mother—she was fourteen years old when she became pregnant with her son. However, her son was born prematurely and did not live long.

Winfrey's life began to turn around when she was once again sent to Nashville, this time in high school, and her father encouraged her to prioritize her education. It was soon recognized that Winfrey was a gifted speaker, which ultimately led her to earn a scholarship to Tennessee State University. During her senior year of high school, Winfrey began her media career when she did the news part-time for the local black radio station. Winfrey later became the youngest news anchor and the first black female news anchor at a Nashville television station. She moved her way up through jobs in the news industry before launching her talk show, *The Oprah Winfrey Show*, in 1986.

From there, her career skyrocketed and made her into the incredibly successful media mogul, talk show host, actress, producer, and philanthropist she is today. Winfrey had a gift for connecting with guests on her talk show and for connecting with the audience. That powerful combination brought her incredible success and allowed her to branch out into the entertainment and philanthropy fields she wanted to explore.

GIVING BACK

Oprah Winfrey has given away hundreds of millions of dollars to charitable causes. From 2004 to 2010, she was listed among the top 50 philanthropists in the United States. She was the first black person to ever make the list. In 2013, she gave $12 million to the Smithsonian National Museum of African American History and Culture. In 2007, she opened the Winfrey Leadership Academy for Girls in South Africa, in which she invested $40 million and much time and effort.

Chapter 2
Racial Diversity in Business

There is a lack of racial diversity in US businesses. In 2014, the United States Census Bureau found that only 17.5 percent of US businesses were owned by minorities.

Unemployment

The lack of racial diversity in businesses is not surprising, given the high overall rates of unemployment for minorities. In 2016, the Bureau of Labor Statistics (BLS) found that while the national unemployment rate was 4.9 percent, Native Americans had an unemployment rate of 8.9 percent and black people had a rate of 8.4 percent. Asian and white citizens both had unemployment rates below the national average, while the rate for unemployed Hispanic citizens was slightly above the national average.

Minority Statistics for Men in Business-Related Occupations

According to the BLS, 40 percent of white men working in the United States are employed in management, professional, and related occupations—that is, mostly in the business field. However, only 30 percent of black men are employed in this sector, as well as only 22 percent of Hispanic men.

Black and Hispanic men are outnumbered by white men in management and professional occupations.

Racial Diversity in Business

Asians have the highest percentage for this set of statistics: 52 percent of Asian men employed are working in management, professional, and related occupations.

Statistics for Women in Business-Related Occupations

The statistics look a little different for women. Among employed Asian women, 51 percent worked in management, professional, and related occupations. For white women, the number was 44 percent. The percentage for black women was higher than for black men, too: 35 percent. For Hispanic women, the number was also higher than for men: 27 percent.

Based on these statistics, it seems that minority women may have slightly more opportunities to work in business-related fields than minority men. That is simply based on racial breakdown, though. Business is a highly male-dominated field. According to a United States Census Bureau report published in 2016, women owned less than 20 percent of all businesses in the United States. So, the business sector is largely dominated by men, but when looking at the racial breakdown, it seems that there is a higher percentage of minority women in the business field than there is of minority men.

Female minorities have a slightly better chance of working in business-related fields than male minorities.

CRITICAL THINKING QUESTION: Why do you think there may be more opportunity for female minorities than male minorities in business positions in the United States?

Diversity in Business

Expanding the Talent Pool

In 2015, consulting firm McKinsey & Company analyzed 366 companies. It found that those with the highest rates of racial and ethnic diversity were 35 percent more likely to have financial returns that were above the national median. In other words, the most racially diverse companies had higher profits than the less racially diverse companies. McKinsey & Company repeated its analysis in 2017 and found the numbers to be much the same: More racially diverse companies still saw better financial returns than less racially diverse companies.

McKinsey & Company suggested that by being more open to having a racially diverse workforce, businesses were able to recruit the most talented people in the field. That is a common finding among different occupational fields: When the pool of potential applicants is bigger (because certain groups are not excluded), more talented people are able to be recruited.

Top-Down Approach

Shellye Archambeau, Chief Executive Officer (CEO) of MetricStream, is one of the few black female CEOs in the technology field. Archambeau points out that it is not enough to encourage racial diversity in lower-level jobs at a company. For a company to see real benefit from a diverse workforce, there needs to be racial diversity in leadership positions, too. When a company hires racially diverse people for low-level jobs, it can be a matter of the

Only 30 percent of black men in the United States are employed in business-related fields.

Racial Diversity in Business

Diverse teams can bring energy and fresh ideas to the table.

company basically filling a quota—wanting to appear diverse, even when the company is actually run by a particular majority group, such as white or Asian businesspeople. When a company is racially diverse in management and leadership positions, too, it has the benefit of taking advantage of the unique talents and viewpoints that a diverse pool of people brings.

Embracing Racial Diversity

Tech companies, which are some of the most profitable ones, are known for not being particularly diverse, either racially or with regard to gender. However, certain large tech companies have begun to recognize the benefits of encouraging racial diversity and are actively promoting a more racially diverse workforce. These companies include Apple, Google, and Facebook. Hopefully, they will inspire a shift in the US business field.

CRITICAL THINKING QUESTION: What unique viewpoints do you think minorities can bring to leadership roles in business?

Diversity in Business

Ursula Burns:
One of the World's Most Powerful Women

Ursula Burns was born in the 1950s and raised by a single mother with limited means. She spent her childhood years growing up in a housing project in New York City. Like Oprah Winfrey, she has gone on to find great success in business, despite the fact that she comes from humble beginnings.

Burns attended an all-girls Catholic school in New York, thanks to her mother's careful budgeting. There, she says she was trained to be one of three things: a nun, a nurse, or a teacher. However, Burns had other aspirations. She wanted to become an engineer. She obtained her bachelor's degree in mechanical engineering from Brooklyn Polytechnic (now New York University Tandon School of Engineering), where she was one of very few women—and even fewer black women—among a lot of white men. She earned her master's degree from Columbia University in 1981.

Ursula Burns's business acumen led her to be highly successful. She was the first black woman to run a Fortune 500 company.

14

Racial Diversity in Business

A Life-Changing Job

During the year between completing her bachelor's degree and starting her master's program, Burns worked as a summer intern at Xerox, a print company. She joined the company's product development and planning department full time after completing her master's degree. For some, it might just have been a first job but for Burns, it was life-changing. In 2009, she became the first black woman CEO of a Fortune 500 company when she took the lead at Xerox. She stayed in that role until December 2016, though she remained on the board of directors until mid-2017. During her time as CEO, Burns led Xerox through a major corporate acquisition, which allowed them to become a true technology services enterprise.

Dreaming Big

In 2009, President Barack Obama appointed Burns to help lead the White House National Science, Technology, Engineering, and Math (STEM) program. Burns continued in the position until 2016. Today, Burns serves on several boards of directors, including Boston Scientific, University of Rochester, American Express, Exxon Mobil, Nestlé, and Uber.

She is also active in organizations that help women and minorities gain education and confidence so they can, as she says, "dream big." Currently, she is encouraging women to enter the tech industry, which has long been dominated by men.

As the first black female CEO of a Fortune 500 company, Burns has been very visible in the business world. Forbes has named her one of the 100 most powerful women in the world multiple times.

THE FORTUNE 500
The Fortune 500 is a list created annually by *Fortune* magazine. Using total revenue as its basis, it lists the 500 largest corporations in the United States. The list began in 1955 and is widely used as a marker in the business industry, even though there are also Fortune 100 and Fortune 1000 lists. Earning a place on the Fortune 500 is a feather in the cap of a large corporation.

Chapter 3
Gender Diversity in Business

Although the gender gap in business is narrowing and the benefits of having women in leadership positions in business are well recognized, the business field still has more men than women.

According to Catalyst, a nonprofit agency that promotes the inclusion of women in the workplace, women-owned businesses make up fewer than 20 percent of all US operations. As of 2017, there were only twenty-six women holding the CEO position at S&P 500 companies—which equates to only 5.2 percent of CEOs at these companies being female. Notable examples include Mary Barra, the CEO of General Motors; Marillyn Hewson, the CEO of Lockheed; and Geisha Williams, the CEO of Pacific Gas & Electric (PG&E). Still, female CEOs of major companies are few and far between.

In Fortune 500 companies, the numbers are even smaller. A 2015 article in the *New York Times* pointed out that only 4.1 percent of Fortune 500 CEOs were women, while 4.5 percent were men named David and 5.3 percent were men named John. In other words, a Fortune 500 company is more likely to be run by men named David or John than it is to be run by a female CEO.

Though more and more women are joining the business sector, the number of women in high positions, such as CEO, is still quite low.

Interestingly though, more women than men earned college degrees in 2015. The difference was slight, but 30.2 percent of women earned a four-year college degree, while 29.9 percent of men did.

What accounts for this lack of women in high positions in business? According to a report by Women in the Workplace, men are 30 percent more likely than women to be promoted from entry-level jobs to management jobs. And a Pew Research study found that 40 percent of Americans think that there is a double standard against hiring women. They found that people believed that both men and women were more likely to hire men rather than women.

Financial Benefits of Gender Diversity

According to McKinsey & Company, though, gender diversity is a distinct benefit in business. The firm's 2015 study found that the most gender-diverse companies were 15 percent more likely to have financial returns greater than the national industry median. They also found that the companies with the least gender diversity were the most likely to lag behind the national industry median.

CRITICAL THINKING QUESTION: What factors can you think of that might account for the relatively low numbers of women in high positions in business?

With gender diversity there are typically higher revenues for businesses.

Diversity in Business

Expanding the Talent Pool

Much like embracing racial diversity expands the talent pool from which businesses can hire people, so does encouraging gender diversity. The breakdown of men and women in the United States changes constantly, but it is usually close to a 50/50 split. This means that if businesses limit much of their hiring to men, they are excluding roughly half of the population. It makes sense that when the hiring pool is expanded to include both men and women, businesses can pick and choose the most talented, qualified people.

Positive Business Metrics

Metrics are criteria that can be measured. In business, common metrics are productivity, profitability, employee commitment and retention, and quality of products or services. In 2014, Gallup, an organization that studies business and leadership, studied more than eight hundred businesses in the retail and hospitality fields. It found that gender-diverse businesses had significantly higher revenues and profits than non-diverse businesses. It also found that gender-diverse businesses in which employees were strongly engaged, meaning they cared about the business and put a strong effort into their work, had dramatically higher revenues and profits.

Scientific American published an article in 2014 (and updated it in 2017) showing that employees in diverse workplaces had stronger engagement. In other words, diversity brings engagement, and engagement brings much higher revenue and profit for any business.

Employees who work together in diverse environments are usually more engaged in their work.

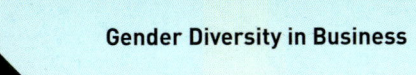

Women make up a significant portion of the consumer marketplace, making the contributions of women in business even more important.

Companies that employ both men and women in leadership roles experience greater success because they are diverse. This diversity brings greater engagement.

Employee retention is another metric often studied. According to the Forté Foundation, a nonprofit collection of leading businesses and top business schools that aims to create more inclusive business workplaces for women, companies with a culture of inclusion have better employee retention—they have fewer employees quitting or being fired.

Another business metric is sales or profit. To make a profit, businesses need customers. Given that women make up roughly half of the population, it makes sense that to appeal to as many consumers as possible, the business needs to market to both men and women. In fact, it may be even *more* important to market to women, depending on the business. Studies have shown that women often influence more decisions about buying than men do. Having a gender-diverse business means that the business has insight into what will appeal to female consumers, which will ultimately increase the company's profits.

CRITICAL THINKING QUESTION:

Why do you think women might make the majority of buying decisions in the United States?

Diversity in Business

Sheryl Sandberg:

Facebook's COO

Sheryl Sandberg is one of the most powerful businesspeople in the United States. She has been on *Time's* annual list of the 100 most influential people in the world, and she is worth more than $1 billion. Sandberg is the chief operating officer (COO) of Facebook and holds the distinction of being the first woman to serve on Facebook's board of directors. Sandberg is perhaps best known, though, for launching the Lean In movement and founding the Lean In Foundation.

Leaning In

The Lean In movement takes its name from Sandberg's 2013 book, *Lean In: Women, Work, and the Will to Lead.* The book describes the barriers women face in business and government leadership positions. Some of the barriers include issues such as gender discrimination and harassment.

Sheryl Sandberg is the founder of the Lean In movement, which aims to empower all women in business.

Gender Diversity in Business

Sandberg also suggests that women themselves create some of the barriers by taking on the gender roles that generations of US men and women have enforced. That is, women have long been seen as homemakers and caretakers, and even now that many women are in the workforce, they still take on the role of primary homemaker and caretaker, which leaves them unable to really move up into business leadership roles.

The Lean In movement has been embraced by many, but it also has many critics. Some people say Sandberg cannot really speak as the voice of most women, because she grew up privileged. Her father was an ophthalmologist and her mother was a college professor, so the family was comfortable financially. Sandberg excelled in high school, was a National Honor Society member, and was accepted into Harvard University. She graduated *summa cum laude* and with a prestigious award for being the top graduating student in economics. She went on to also earn her Master of Business Administration (MBA) from Harvard, with highest honors.

Sandberg may have been privileged but she has also worked hard to secure her position in the business world. Her late husband was also a powerful business executive, but the two shared parenting duties to raise their son and daughter, so that both could continue their careers. Sandberg's husband died unexpectedly but Sandberg has the determination to face the challenges that come along with single parenting and being a leading COO.

FACEBOOK AND DIVERSITY
Facebook has an incredibly diverse user base. As such, the company has recognized the need to improve its workforce diversity. In 2017, women made up 21 percent of all new technical hires at Facebook, as well as 27 percent of all new engineering-graduate hires. That same year, it increased the percentage of Hispanic employees from 4 percent to 5 percent and black employees from 2 percent to 3 percent. While these numbers are still quite low, Facebook is committed to improving its diversity.

Chapter 4
Economic and Social Diversity in Business

While we have seen that it is possible to come from a poor background and succeed in the business world, rags-to-riches stories like those of Oprah Winfrey and Ursula Burns are not common.

Children from disadvantaged families often do not get the schooling and opportunities that could help them break the cycle of poverty.

Economic and Social Diversity in Business

CRITICAL THINKING QUESTION: Why do you think it is important for young women and men to see people who grew up in similarly difficult circumstances succeeding in business?

A Rough Beginning

Marah Lidey is the cofounder of Shine, an organization that encourages mindfulness among professionals. Lidey grew up in a home where there was not much money to spare. Her family often relied on food stamps and the Dollar Menu at McDonald's for food. Lidey's stepfather was in and out of jail. Nevertheless, she feels that her life experiences are part of what has made her who she is: a hard worker who is empathetic, strong, and kind. However, she also admits that those same life experiences were not the kind of thing one would put on their résumé. This is why Lidey is invested in trying to improve socioeconomic diversity in business. She is one of the lucky ones who recognized her own ability and made a successful career for herself, but she worries that other young women who grow up in situations like hers may not realize the opportunities they can pursue. If young women from difficult upbringings do not see women like them in business, Lidey worries they will not realize such a career is possible.

A Needed Perspective

One benefit of having people from diverse socioeconomic backgrounds in business is that they bring much-needed perspective to business operations. For example, it is common in the business world for companies to tell employees, "Just pay for your business travel, and we'll reimburse you." That may be fine for people who have the money, but people who have come from economically challenged backgrounds may be living paycheck to paycheck, unable to front the money and wait for reimbursement. This could create a difficult situation in the workplace, so it is important for employees who have that perspective to be on hand to ensure that no one is put in an uncomfortable position.

Better Customer Relations

Having people from diverse socioeconomic backgrounds in business also helps companies better relate to their customers. Some companies market only to wealthy clients, but most companies market to a wide range of customers—and not all are wealthy or middle-class. So, to understand the needs and circumstances of its customers, a business can benefit from having people on staff who are very familiar with the challenges that some customers face and what unique needs they have.

Diversity in Business

Increasing the Candidate Pool

Marah Lidey suggests that to improve socioeconomic diversity in business, businesses should start actively recruiting from a wider pool of applicants. Currently, major businesses often recruit from top colleges or from people in the local area. Local people may come from diverse backgrounds, but people from top colleges often come from upper-middle-class or wealthy backgrounds. If companies looked at people from more affordable colleges or even at teens from at-risk neighborhoods who could perhaps be shepherded through their education and groomed to work in the business, it would be a big step toward increasing socioeconomic diversity.

Hiring people from varied backgrounds is just the first step, though. Once they are hired, the company must create an environment of inclusion so that all employees feel comfortable and can work together. Otherwise, the employees who do not feel comfortable—most likely the employees from more challenging backgrounds—are unlikely to stay with the company. Businesses run best when they have a low turnover of staff, so creating an inclusive workplace can be good for the business overall.

Scouting potential employees from more affordable colleges can increase diversity in the applicant pool.

Economic and Social Diversity in Business

CRITICAL THINKING QUESTION: What are some ways businesses can create an environment of inclusion?

Encouraging Diversity in Entrepreneurship

Business is not just working for a company. It also includes entrepreneurship. A study by researchers from Duke University, the University of Akron, and the University of Southern California found that more than 90 percent of entrepreneurs were people from middle-class or higher backgrounds and had more education. The same study found that 73 percent of entrepreneurs had relied on their network connections in business to build their companies. In other words, an economically challenged person with no real contacts in the business world is not very likely to start a business.

Lidey points out that part of the reason people from poorer backgrounds are unlikely entrepreneurs is that they simply have not had the time to devote to it. These people are sometimes struggling to feed themselves and their families and to keep a stable roof over their head. That consumes all their energy, and they barely have time to think about how they could start a business—much less the money needed to start one. Undoubtedly some of these people have good ideas and could, with appropriate support, build good businesses. So, in the interest of improving the business field, it would be wise to encourage people from diverse socioeconomic backgrounds to explore entrepreneurship and potentially build businesses of their own.

Anyone can have a great idea, but it takes money and opportunity to turn that idea into a business.

25

Diversity in Business

Howard Schultz:
CEO of Starbucks

Howard Schultz earned his fortune as the CEO of Starbucks coffee company. Although he resigned as CEO in 2017, Schultz remains the executive chairman of the multibillion-dollar coffee company.

Schultz was not raised in a wealthy family. He was born in 1953 to a truck-driver father, Fred, who dropped out of high school, and his mother Elaine, who raised the children. The family lived in a housing project in Brooklyn. When Schultz was eight years old, his father broke his leg and hip. The family did not have insurance, and Schultz's father lost his job. Their financial situation went from bad to worse, with Schultz and his two younger siblings living in poverty.

Keeping the Faith

Schultz's mother, though, never lost faith that her children could climb out of poverty. She told Schultz that he would go to college, and indeed he did. Schultz won a football scholarship to Northern Michigan University, where he studied communications. After college, he briefly worked for Xerox and then became general manager for a company that made coffee makers. While there, he noticed

ENVIRONMENTALLY FRIENDLY

Starbucks is taking steps to be more environmentally friendly. In 1999, it began giving used coffee grounds to people for use in personal compost piles. In 2008, the company began using cup sleeves made from 85 percent recycled fiber. In 2009, it developed a new dipper-well system to decrease the amount of water wasted while rinsing utensils. In addition to environmentally friendly practices, Starbucks has worked to support farmer equity, fair trade, clean water, and decrease hunger in the United States.

Economic and Social Diversity in Business

 that a small coffee-roasting company, Starbucks, was ordering more coffee makers than some of their large clients so he decided to visit Starbucks.

Schultz had visited Milan, Italy, in 1981, where coffeehouses were like bars—people gathered there to socialize. When he saw the popularity of Starbucks' coffee beans, he had the idea that perhaps Starbucks could become the US version of those Italian coffeehouses he had seen.

Schultz's mother, who was so proud that her son had graduated college, was dismayed when he left his general manager job to join Starbucks. At that time in the United States, people made their own coffee at home or ordered a cup in a restaurant where they were eating. There were no places where people went solely to buy expensive coffee and socialize.

Schultz was right to follow his dream. Starbucks now operates more than twenty-seven thousand stores worldwide, and its revenue in 2017 was more than $22 billion. Schultz has never forgotten his own family's struggles, though. Starbucks became one of the first companies in the United States to offer free healthcare coverage to part-time employees. Schultz says that move was inspired by his father's experience when he was injured. He wanted to build a company that would honor people like his father—as he says, a company "with a conscience."

Schultz built Starbucks into a company that respects its employees as well as the environment. In 2006, Starbucks began using 10 percent recycled paper in their hot-drink cups.

Chapter 5
Cultural Diversity in Business

The United States has long been known as a cultural melting pot. And for good reason: when the United States was first established, it was home to Native Americans and European, British, and Mexican immigrants. Each group brought its own cultures and customs.

International markets are one place where the cultural diversity of the United States is readily apparent.

What Is Culture?

The word "culture" refers to the arts, achievements, social institutions, and customs of a particular group of people. It is not the same as "race," although sometimes culture goes hand in hand with race. For example, in the United States there is black culture, Latinx culture, Asian culture, and so on. But within those large, race-based groups, there are smaller cultural divisions. For example, some Asian families living in the United States consider themselves mainly American, while others still remain closely connected to their Asian cultural heritage.

Understanding Customers

Businesses exist to serve customers—either with services or with products. In the United States, the customer base is usually made up of people from many different cultures.

There are some businesses that market specifically to certain cultures, of course. For example, some traditional Asian stores market mostly to people from Asian cultures. However, they get customers from other cultures, too. And larger businesses typically exist to serve customers from many cultures.

> **CRITICAL THINKING QUESTION:**
> What are some cultural groups other than those mentioned that you know of in the United States?

For a business to have a good understanding of its customers and their needs and wants, it is important that the business understands the cultures it is serving. And while anyone can read about cultural customs and learn something, there are subtle cultural differences that a business might miss if they do not have employees who are familiar with that culture. For example, in some Middle Eastern countries, the left hand is used for hygiene—such as cleaning oneself after using the restroom. So, in business dealings, it is considered extremely rude to use the left hand to shake hands or pass documents back and forth. And if the business meeting involves a meal, it is most definitely considered rude to use the left hand to eat. In Finland, it is not unusual for business to be conducted while steaming in a sauna—which would feel extremely unfamiliar to Americans, given that one wears little clothing while in a sauna.

Cultural awareness is critical in a global business market.

Diversity in Business

A business staffed only with people from a particular cultural background may be unaware of cultural subtleties, and it could negatively affect its business dealings. Cultural awareness is becoming more and more important as business is increasingly conducted, with companies all over the world. The European Commission (EC) did a study on two hundred companies in 2003, and found that having a diverse workforce led to better trust in a company from a culturally diverse customer base.

Innovation is important to businesses, too. If businesses do not create and innovate, they may stagnate and die. Automobile giant Daimler/Chrysler found that the most successful product-development teams were made up of diverse groups of people. They formed teams with both genders and a wide variety of ages, and no more than half of the team was from one specific culture. That diversity provided product-development teams with a wide view of the marketplace and what customers' needs might be.

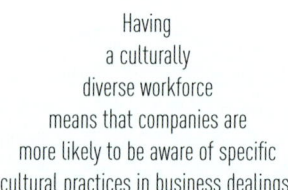

Having a culturally diverse workforce means that companies are more likely to be aware of specific cultural practices in business dealings.

Economic Benefits to Culturally Diverse Businesses

There are definite economic benefits to companies that are culturally diverse. DiversityInc. conducts an annual study on the most diverse companies, and it recently found that the fifty most diverse companies made up just 7 percent of the Fortune 500 companies, but they generated 22 percent of the total revenue of all the companies on the list. In other words, a very small number of companies generated a huge portion of Fortune 500 revenue—and those companies happened to be among the most culturally diverse.

Cultural Diversity in Business

Companies that have created strong culturally diverse workforces include Google, Daimler/Chrysler, and Johnson and Johnson.

The 2003 EC report also found that the more diverse a company is, the lower the staff turnover and the less the company's legal expenses. From a legal standpoint, a culturally diverse company does not face possible lawsuits for wrongful hiring and firing practices based on cultural discrimination. And a company that values cultural diversity tends to have loyal employees who are likely to stay with the company for longer.

Communication Is Key

It is one thing to hire a culturally diverse workforce, but it is another to retain them and ensure a strong working environment. Companies that embrace cultural diversity have found that communication is vital. If stereotypes exist, they must be addressed. If different goals exist based on cultural differences, that must be reconciled, too. For a business to succeed, employees must be comfortable in the workplace, and communication is a good way to ensure that.

CRITICAL THINKING QUESTION: What sorts of cultural stereotypes do you think might come up in business, and how might they be addressed?

Diversity in Business

Sergey Brin:
Cofounder of Google

Sergey Brin, the cofounder of tech giant Google, was born in Moscow in 1973. At that time, Russia was part of the Soviet Union—a socialist empire that existed from 1922 to 1991. When Brin was born, the Soviet Union, led by Leonid Brezhnev, was in the middle of the Cold War. Under Brezhnev, the Soviet Union experienced much corruption and socioeconomic hardship. Brezhnev was determined to make the Soviet Union a military superpower, and that meant the rest of the Soviet economy suffered.

During the Cold War, the Soviet Union and the United States were engaged in a nuclear arms race to see who could develop the most powerful nuclear weapons in the event of another world war. So, there was always the threat that nuclear war between the two superpowers could break out.

From Russia to Maryland

In 1979 Brin's father, Michael, decided that the family had to leave the Soviet Union. The economy was struggling, and independent thought was not particularly appreciated. Michael was a mathematics professor, but academic intellect was not valued at that time in the Soviet Union—at least, not when the academics were Jewish, as Brin's family is. Brin's parents, both

MORE THAN A SEARCH ENGINE
Google may be best known as a search engine, but the company also develops other technologies. Gmail is Google's email platform. Google Maps is a mapping application, Google Photos is a photo organizing and editing suite, and Google+ is Google's answer to social media. The company is also working on fiber optics, WiFi, and virtual reality.

Cultural Diversity in Business

According to *Forbes*, Sergey Brin is the thirteenth-richest person in the world.

> university-educated professionals, faced anti-Semitism in school and then in the workplace. The Brins ended up being among the last Jews allowed to leave the Soviet Union until Mikhail Gorbachev took power in the late 1980s.

The Brin family moved to Maryland, where Sergey had difficulty starting school given his inability to speak English. Sergey was shy but smart and self-confident. He did well in school once he mastered the language: he completed high school in three years, and college in three years, too. He earned degrees in math and computer science and graduated near the top of his class.

After winning a National Science Foundation (NSF) scholarship, Sergey went to Stanford University to earn his PhD. However, he never finished that degree. During orientation at Stanford, Brin met Larry Page and the two went on to found Google in the late 1990s.

Today, in addition to his work with Google, Brin has become a philanthropist with an eye toward working on the climate and energy problems facing the world.

Chapter 6
Diverse Abilities in Business

According to the United States Census Bureau, approximately 19 percent of people in the United States have a disability. That is nearly one in five people!

Disability Breakdown

"Disability" is a term that describes a wide range of conditions. The Centers for Disease Control (CDC) has further broken down what those disabilities look like. According to the CDC in 2015, approximately 53 million adults in the United States were living with a disability, which translated to 22 percent of adults. (The Census Bureau's 19 percent includes children, too.)

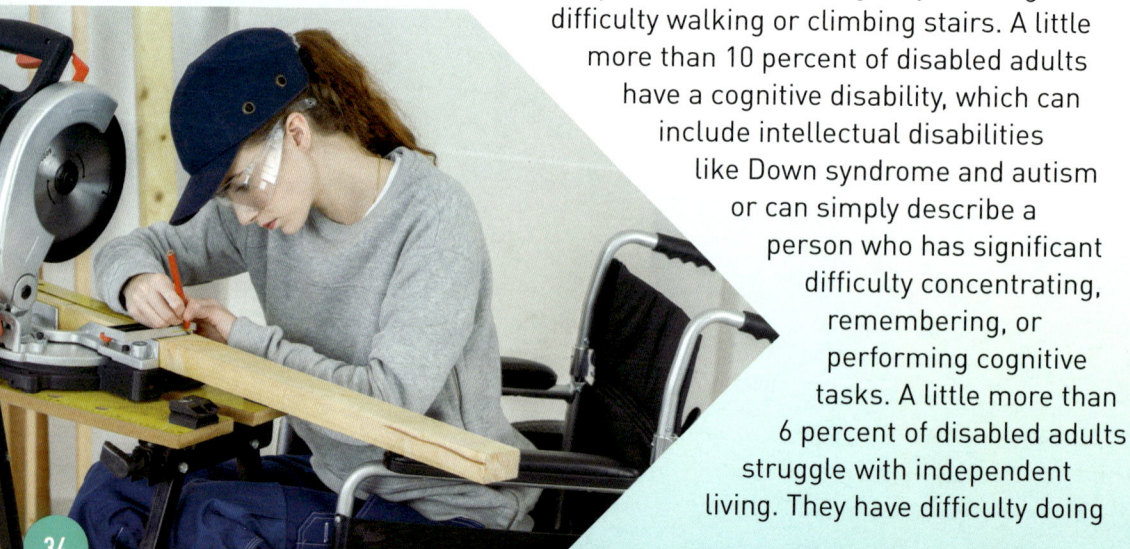

Today, people with disabilities are able to do more jobs than were available to them in the past.

The CDC broke down the percentage of functional disabilities—in other words, disabilities that were not severe enough to require adults to be institutionalized or require one-on-one care all day, every day. The CDC found that 13 percent of disabled adults in the United States have a mobility limitation, meaning they have significant difficulty walking or climbing stairs. A little more than 10 percent of disabled adults have a cognitive disability, which can include intellectual disabilities like Down syndrome and autism or can simply describe a person who has significant difficulty concentrating, remembering, or performing cognitive tasks. A little more than 6 percent of disabled adults struggle with independent living. They have difficulty doing errands or performing daily tasks without help. Blindness or serious visual impairments accounted for 4.6 percent of adults with disabilities, and 3.6 percent had significant difficulty dressing or bathing themselves. Interestingly, the CDC research also found that certain states, particularly in the South, had the highest rates of disability. Chronic diseases such as diabetes and heart disease are more common in the South, so it is thought that may account for the higher rates of disability in those states.

The CDC research also found that certain minority groups, such as Hispanic and black people, were more likely to have disabilities. And people with less education, lower income, or who are unemployed were also more likely to be disabled. The reasons for this are complex, but they are all linked to the fact that people from ethnic minority groups or lower-income groups are less likely to have access to good healthcare than people from non-minority groups.

The Americans with Disabilities Act

Today, these statistics mean less than they used to. Many people with disabilities are perfectly capable of working—and many want to work. With the 1990 passage of the Americans with Disabilities Act (ADA), working became a more attainable goal for people with disabilities.

People with intellectual disabilities are now able to work in office jobs, in competitive integrated employment.

CRITICAL THINKING QUESTION: What value do you think people with disabilities could add to a workplace?

Diversity in Business

From a physical standpoint, ADA requires public and private businesses to improve accessibility. Businesses had to remove architectural barriers that prevented people with mobility limitations from entering. For example, buildings that were previously accessible only by stairs had to add wheelchair ramps. Businesses are also required to allow service animals, such as guide dogs for the blind and hearing dogs for the deaf, on their premises. Public transportation also had to make their services accessible for people with disabilities.

ADA ensures that all public and private businesses are accessible to people with disabilities. That includes having disabled-accessible restrooms.

On a larger scale, the passage of ADA meant that schools and businesses could no longer discriminate against people with disabilities when hiring employees, training them, advancing them in jobs, or even firing them. For job-application and retention purposes, ADA states that people with disabilities should have the same rights as nondisabled people.

The Individuals with Disabilities Education Act

The same year that ADA was signed into law, the Individuals with Disabilities Education Act (IDEA) was also passed. IDEA states that students with disabilities must be provided with a free and appropriate public education (FAPE) in the least restrictive environment (LRE), with appropriate supports. Previously, many students with disabilities were put in segregated "life skills" types of classroom, where they were never around typically developing students, and they learned skills like toileting, dressing, and simple life skills, rather than being allowed to learn what nondisabled students in US schools learn. Not surprisingly, this set students with disabilities up for failure in the job market. Without the education others had access to, students with disabilities were not able to get meaningful, competitive jobs. And as recently as the 1980s, students who were considered to have more serious disabilities, such as

Diverse Abilities in Business

Down syndrome, were often institutionalized and given no education. IDEA was put in place to change that. A FAPE in the LRE is legally considered to be an education alongside typical, nondisabled peers in a mainstream classroom—with supports to help students with disabilities be successful. For example, some students with disabilities have aides, some have homework and classwork modifications, and so on.

The passage of ADA and IDEA has resulted in people with disabilities earning an education and having the opportunity to access jobs. And that, in turn, has resulted in more people with diverse abilities working in US business.

IDEA ensures that students with disabilities are given the chance to earn a meaningful education, which will prepare them for the workforce.

Diversity in Business

Benefits of Employing People with Disabilities

Welcoming people with diverse abilities into the workforce widens the applicant pool. If one in five Americans has a disability, employers miss out on approximately 20 percent of the potential employees in the United States when they do not consider hiring people with disabilities. Many people with disabilities have much to offer in the workplace, and companies that recognize this are able to add valuable employees to their workforce. For example, tech giant Microsoft has launched an initiative to hire people with autism. Autism is considered to be a developmental disability and sometimes an intellectual disability, but many people now recognize it as a neurodiversity—that is, autistic people are not disabled, they simply think differently from others. That different way of thinking often works well for computer programmers and others in the tech field, and companies like Microsoft recognize the value and talent neurodiverse employees can bring to the company.

Microsoft actively recruits people with autism, recognizing the strong contributions they can make in the tech field.

CRITICAL THINKING QUESTION: Can you think of other jobs that neurodiverse people might be well suited for? What do you think would make them particularly well suited for those jobs?

Diverse Abilities in Business

People with disabilities are also known for being reliable employees who have a high rate of retention. In other words, when they get a good job, they tend to stick with it and be reliable about showing up to work. Perhaps this is because the unemployment rate for people with disabilities is more than double that of people without disabilities—so people with disabilities often know that if they lose a job, it may be difficult for them to find another one.

Diversity in the workforce is always a benefit, too. Numerous studies have shown that businesses with diversity—whether it is regarding race, gender, socioeconomic status, culture, or ability—have greater rates of creativity and innovation, which often translates into stronger revenue. In business, it is extremely common for people to work in teams. When teams are made up of a diverse group of individuals, more viewpoints and ideas are brought to the table, and sometimes those differing viewpoints and perspectives can lead to amazing and profitable results.

Many people with disabilities require only minimal accommodations to perform the same types of jobs as everyone else.

Diversity in Business

Richard Branson:
Dyslexic Business Tycoon

Dyslexia did not stop Richard Branson from building a highly successful business empire.

Some disabilities are considered learning disabilities. They may or may not affect a person's future employment, but they can make learning quite difficult in school. One fairly common learning disability is dyslexia. Dyslexia describes any learning disability that involves learning to read or interpret words, letters, numbers, or other symbols. People with dyslexia usually have a normal intelligence level but they struggle with reading and decoding tasks. Dyslexia can be relatively mild or can be quite severe.

British businessman and philanthropist Richard Branson has dyslexia and performed poorly throughout his school career. But he was bright and had a lot of potential. In fact, his school headmaster once told him that he would either end up in prison or become a millionaire! The latter turned out to be true—and then some. As of November 2017, Branson was worth an estimated $5.1 billion, according to *Forbes* magazine.

Diverse Abilities in Business

A Different Way of Thinking

Branson's first business was a magazine called *Student*. He was just sixteen years old when he started it. By the time he was twenty-two, he had opened a chain of record stores called Virgin Records. Virgin Records became Virgin Megastores, and Branson expanded the Virgin brand into a music label (Virgin Records), an airline (Virgin Atlantic), and a wireless communications company (Virgin Mobile), among other endeavors. Branson's music label was his initial big venture, and it was wildly successful. Branson signed such big-name artists as the Rolling Stones, Culture Club, and Paula Abdul.

Not only does Branson not see his dyslexia as a drawback, he believes dyslexia should be seen as a sign of potential. Much like some people consider autism to be a neurodiversity, Branson says dyslexia is simply a different way of thinking. In fact, he says it allowed him to think more creatively and to see solutions where other people saw problems. He also says people with dyslexia often simplify things, which can lead to better problem-solving.

Branson notes that being dyslexic can give people an advantage in business; people with dyslexia are often great verbal communicators because they have had to rely on speech rather than the written word. Entrepreneus with dyslexia work well with people and generally enjoy teamwork, which helps them build a successful business with a happy workforce. Branson feels that being dyslexic made him a better manager, and given that he manages a massive business empire, it is easy to see why he considers dyslexia a strength, not a drawback.

VIRGIN AMERICA

There are a number of Virgin-branded airlines, including Virgin Atlantic, Virgin Australia, and Virgin America. However, Virgin America planes may not be seen in the United States for much longer. The airline began in 2007 but was sold to the Alaska Air Group, which operates Alaska Airlines and Horizon Airlines, in 2016. They plan to discontinue Virgin America by 2018. It is not a huge loss to the Virgin Group, however, which has businesses in spaceflight, retail, consumer electronics, banking, multimedia, jewelry, healthcare, and travel, too.

Diversity in Business

Benefits of Diversity

Business is a fast-paced world that relies on innovation and creativity, interpersonal skills, management skills, and knowledge of the particular market, just to name a few skills. Diversity can help in all of these areas.

Numerous studies have shown that when diverse groups of people work together, creativity and innovation are greater. That stands true regardless of whether the group is culturally diverse, racially diverse, economically diverse, or diverse in gender or ability. More minds, more perspectives, and more varied backgrounds lead to different ways of looking at problems and solutions, which leads to better innovation and problem-solving.

Interpersonal and managerial skills are extremely important in business. Business deals are often influenced by the relationships formed between people. When a company embraces diversity, its leadership and employees learn more about people with different backgrounds and generally develop more respect and tolerance for others. That can translate into better interpersonal skills, because they have learned how to relate well to different people. Managerial skills are equally important in business. Employees rarely stay at a company with poor management. If a manager is unskilled, uninterested, or just plain rude, he or she will not inspire the best work from employees. And, in fact, employees often leave for jobs at other places, where the management is stronger.

According to the United States Census Bureau, the country will continue to grow in diversity in the coming decades.

Diverse Abilities in Business

Market knowledge is important, too. For example, sales businesses need to know the needs and wants of their potential customers. If they are unaware of the specific needs of a particular group of customers, they are likely to lose those potential customers. Having a diverse team increases the chances that the business will be aware of factors affecting the buying decisions of many groups of potential customers.

A Shift to Come

The United States is an incredibly diverse country. According to the United States Census Bureau, it is likely that by 2044 white people will make up just a little more than 49 percent of the population. The remaining 51 percent of the population will be made up of all the other represented races combined. Because of this, it is important to recognize that business in the United States will likely shift to reflect the makeup of the country. If, as the Census Bureau believes, 25 percent of Americans will be Hispanic in 2044, then it is likely that businesses will see an increase in Hispanic employees and leaders by that time, too. There are many factors involved, however, including educational opportunities and hiring practices. But wise business owners recognize the value of diversity in the business workplace and embrace the benefits that will come with this shift.

Timeline

1913: Henry Ford of the Ford Motor Company offers to pay immigrants and black people $5 per day to work at his company—twice the amount of the typical daily wage at that time.

1938: The Fair Labor Standards Act is passed, establishing a minimum wage regardless of gender.

1940–1945: Women in the United States increasingly enter the workforce to fill positions vacated by men enlisting in the military to fight in World War II.

1948: President Harry Truman signs Executive Order 9981, which desegregates the military.

1961: President John F. Kennedy signs Executive Order 10925, promoting nondiscriminatory hiring and employment practices.

1963: The Equal Pay Act is passed, in an attempt to close the pay gap between men and women.

1964: The Civil Rights Act is passed, removing barriers to employment for people of color.

1965: President Lyndon B. Johnson signs Executive Order 11246, requiring government employers to enforce nondiscriminatory hiring practices.

1970: INROADS becomes the first organization to directly connect minority students with internships at high-ranked businesses and firms.

1972: Katharine Graham becomes the first female CEO of a Fortune 500 company (the *Washington Post*).

1972: Title IX bans gender discrimination in education programs that receive federal funds.

1978: The Pregnancy Discrimination Act is passed, prohibiting discrimination on the basis of childbirth, pregnancy, or related medical conditions.

1982: For the first time in history, women outnumber men in bachelor's degrees earned from universities.

1984: The Supreme Court rules on *Roberts v. United States Jaycees*, prohibiting public organizations from refusing membership to anyone because of their gender.

1987: Secretary of Labor William Brock commissions the Workforce 2000 study, designed to study and improve diversity in the workplace.

1990: ADA and IDEA are passed, removing barriers to employment and education for people with disabilities.

1993: The Family and Medical Leave Act is passed, providing job protection and leave for family and medical issues.

1994: The Gender Equity in Education Act is passed, establishing programs to train teachers to treat girls and boys equally.

1998: The Supreme Court rules that employers can be held liable for sexual harassment in the workplace.

2009: President Barack Obama signs the Lilly Ledbetter Fair Pay Act, which is intended to reduce the pay gap between men and women.

2011: President Barack Obama adds gender identity and sexual orientation to the Equal Employment Opportunity Commission, preventing employers from discriminating against employees on the basis of gender identity or sexual orientation.

2014: Google becomes the first major tech company to release a diversity report, which it now releases every year.

2014: General Motors becomes the largest company to have a female CEO.

2015: Two major accounting firms, Deloitte and KPMG, name their first female CEOs.

2016: Massachusetts becomes the first state to pass a law requiring that men and women be paid equally for doing comparable work.

Glossary

anti-Semitism Prejudice against Jewish people.
bias Prejudice for or against a person, thing, or group.
cognitive Related to the mental processes of acquiring knowledge.
desegregated Ended racial segregation.
double standard A rule applied in different ways to different people.
empathetic Able to understand and share the feelings of another person.
employee retention The rate at which employees keep their jobs.
entrepreneurship The activity of starting a business.
headmaster The principal of a school.
hijab The head covering worn by some Muslim women in public.
hospitality The business of housing or entertaining visitors.
inclusion The act of including different groups of people within a larger group or structure.
innovation The act of creating something new.
Latinx A gender-inclusive form of the word "Latino," often used by Latinos who are genderqueer.
median The midpoint value in a series of values, where an equal number of values fall above and below it.
mindfulness The state of focusing a person's awareness on the present moment and focusing on calmness.
mogul A powerful or important person.
neurodiversity A range of differences in brain function and behavioral traits, considered part of the normal variation in humans.
revenue A business's income, before expenses.
S&P 500 Acronym for Standard and Poor's 500, a US stock market index.
Silicon Valley The area of Santa Clara County in California that is known for the many computing and electronics businesses headquartered there.
socioeconomic The interaction of social and economic factors.
stereotypes Widely held, often simplified beliefs about a particular type of person or thing.
summa cum laude A Latin term meaning "with highest distinction."

For Further Reading

Books

Bernstein, Daryl. *Better Than a Lemonade Stand: Small Business Ideas for Kids*. New York, NY: Aladdin/Beyond Words, 2012.

Heyward, Andy, and Amy Heyward. *Secret Millionaires Club: Warren Buffett's 26 Secrets to Success in the Business of Life*. Hoboken, NJ: Wiley, 2013.

Toren, Adam, and Matthew Toren. *Kidpreneurs: Young Entrepreneurs with Big Ideas!* Phoenix, AZ: Business Plus Media Group, 2017.

Toren, Adam, and Matthew Toren. *Starting Your Own Business: Become an Entrepreneur!* Hoboken, NJ: Wiley, 2017.

Websites

BizKids
bizkids.com
This interactive site explores business basics.

Lemonade Day
lemonadeday.org
This program explains how to start and operate a business.

Rich Kid Smart Kid
www.richkidsmartkid.com
This interactive website teaches financial lessons and wealth creation.

TheMint
www.themint.org
This fun website sponsored by Northwestern Mutual explores saving and budgeting.

Publisher's note to educators and parents: Our editors have carefully reviewed these websites to ensure that they are suitable for students. Many websites change frequently, however, and we cannot guarantee that a site's future contents will continue to meet our high standards of quality and educational value. Be advised that students should be closely supervised whenever they access the Internet.

Index

Americans with Disabilities Act (ADA) 35, 36, 37
   accessibility 36

bias 7
business owners 4, 11, 16
   women 4, 11, 16
business-related occupations 10–11, 13, 16–17
   women in 11, 16–17

census data 10, 11, 34, 43
CEOs 12, 14–15, 16, 22, 26–27, 40–41
   Archambeau, Shellye 12
   Barra, Mary 16
   Branson, Richard 40–41
   Burns, Ursula 14–15, 22
   Hewson, Marilyn 16
   Schultz, Howard 26–27
   Williams, Geisha 16
Civil Rights Act of 1964 5
cultural awareness 30
cultural background 28, 29
   definition 28
   Middle Eastern 29
customers 6, 19, 23, 28–29, 30, 43

discrimination 5, 36
diversity
   abilities 34–41, 42
      autism 34, 38, 41
      Down syndrome 34, 36
      dyslexia 40–41
      mobility limitations 34
      visual impairment 35
   cultural 28–33, 42
   economic and social 22–27, 42
   gender 7, 16–21, 30, 42
   importance of 6–7, 17, 23, 28–29, 30–31, 38–39, 42–43
      brainstorming 7
      communication 31
      creativity and innovation 7, 30, 39, 42
      decision-making 7
      interpersonal skills 42
      managerial skills 42
   racial 10–16, 18, 42
   workforce 7, 12–13, 30–31

education 15, 16, 25, 26, 27, 33, 35, 36–37, 43
entrepreneurship 25
ethnic background 4, 6, 8, 10, 11, 12, 13, 14–15, 21, 28, 29, 35, 43
   Asian 6, 10, 13, 28, 29
   black 4, 8, 9, 10, 12, 14–15, 21, 28, 35
      female 9, 12, 14–15
   Hispanic/Latinx 10, 11, 21, 28, 35, 43
      women 11
   Native American 4, 10, 28
   white 4, 6, 10, 11, 13, 43
      men 4, 10
      women 11
Executive Order 9981 5

Finland 29
Fortune 500 6, 15, 16, 30

immigrants 4, 28
inclusion, environment of 24, 25
Individuals with Disabilities Education Act (IDEA) 36–37

Lidey, Marah 23, 24

metrics, business 12, 17, 18–19, 24, 30, 31, 39
   employee engagement 18–19
   employee retention 19, 24, 31, 39
   legal expenses 31
   profits 12, 17, 18, 19
   revenue 30, 39
minorities 10, 11, 15
   women 11
Muslims 7

Nike 7

Obama, Barack 8, 15

perspectives 6, 7, 13, 23, 39, 42
philanthropy 9, 33, 40
poverty 6, 8, 22, 23, 25, 26, 35

race, definition 28

S&P 500 16
Starbucks 26–27

talent pool 12–13, 18–19, 24, 38
tech industry 5, 6, 13, 15, 20–21, 32–33, 38, 41
   Apple 13, 41
   Facebook 13, 20–21
      Sandberg, Sheryl 20–21
   Google 6, 13, 32–33
      Brin, Sergey 32–33
      diversity reports 6
      workforce makeup 6
   Microsoft 38
   Silicon Valley 5

unemployment 10, 35, 39

wealth 6, 21, 23, 24
Winfrey, Oprah 8–9, 14, 22
women 6, 8–9, 11, 15, 19, 23
Workforce 2000 study 5

Xerox 15, 26